A DESI GOT ME

RAJ

JUST BAE

ISBN: 978-1-925988-46-8

CONTENTS

His Royal Highness Prince Raj Khatri, wearily climbed up the steps to his partition on the third floor of Nehru Block of Men's Hostels of Engineering College and flopped himself on his bed. His guards were sent away hours ago on orders to leave the young man alone for the evening.

Raj was tired; mentally, physically and psychologically. The first being because of the upcoming midterms he hadn't studied for yet again. He repeated the same in his freshman year and despite passing, Raj felt he was given a helping hand. Physically because of one hour of cricket practice that always went over the time. The coach was worse than a drill sergeant. Psychologically because one, he had to live like an ordinary teenager in spite of being a prince; two, a girl who worked in the registrar had been following him since he arrived. She knew of his royalty stature and always asked if he needed anything. Raj despite trying to avoid her kept bumping into her on the way to his classes throughout the day. He knew she was following her and some of his friends told him to give her a moans-faadu (vagina tearing). Raj did not want to have sex with a woman almost twice his age. He committed himself to marry the Desi girl, Priya, who he paid for to study on campus with him.

It was just five days ago when Raj had come first across that eighteen year old. Her perky little breasts and pointy nipples were on full display as her white blouse didn't mask what was beneath. The freshman never wore a bra. Because of Raj being just Raj, he had no problem approaching her. After they met that morning after their horses mated, the girl had captured the prince's heart. His day and night thoughts of being with her were hard to suppress. He visualized Priya's shy smile held together by her dimples with mischief spelled clearly across her pretty face. The second time they met, though not as intense as the first, still didn't disappoint. Priya let Raj in her dorm room and he kissed, fondled and played with her pussy so much that his hand was dripping cream. Priya reminded him of the agreement they'd made days ago not to have sex before marriage and Raj again complied. The slim long-haired Desi girl then gave Raj a hand job again for the ages that he'd never forget.

Raj laid across his bed thinking of the touch of Priya's delicate fingers jerking him up and down. The look of fascination on her face on seeing his cum erupt was a scene worth rewinding over and over again. The memory gave Raj an instant hard-on. He pulled the pants down seeing his dick had already started oozing pre-cum. Griping the shaft in his fist, Raj crazily started jerking, sliding the wet foreskin on and off its head.

Exhaustion mixed with sweet memories and sweeter sensations lulled him into a state of trance. Now it was the Priya's hand jerking it. He felt it being milked by her moans bringing him on the verge of an intense cumshot. But he was caught off-guard by either the bed making knocking noises or someone knocking?

His trance was broken realizing the knocks, in fact, were coming from the door. Raj pulled up his pants and tried his best to conceal his manhood.

When Raj opened the door, he saw one of the men he most hated in life; none other than Kaniyalal the Karbhari (the chief administrator) of his state of Bansban. The reason being is the following:

When India had become a republic, the kingdoms of the states were divided into Class A, B, and C according to the strength of population with C being the smallest. The state of Bansban was in the level of Class C and Raj was from this class.

Kanaiyalal the Karbhari was a big flunkey. He bent over backwards to fulfill every whim of Raj's father, the King, and of the first queen mother, his stepmother; Pratap Sinh. For the rest of the family, including Raj and his natural mother, Queen Devi, he had nothing but dislike for. His behavior towards his family was border-line disdainful.

The Bansban snake and three others accompanying him bowed before Prince Raj Khatri as customed. Meanwhile, the prince was seething in anger when he uttered, "What do you want?"

Kanaiyalal with all politeness he held in also had a shadow of sorrow on his face. He said, " Oh,

Bapu Saheb (Raj's other name): Maharaja Shri and Maharani Saheba have immediately wish your company in Bansban. These servants along with myself have been sent to escort you."

Raj noticed a black band on the right arm of each of them. "Are Maharaja Shri and Maharani Saheba okay?"

"Yes, Bapu."

"Then, wait for me downstairs. I will be down in a few minutes."

"Yes, Bapu."

Karbhari waved his hand and others left. "Thousand pardons, Bapu Saheb, I am personally ordered by Maharaja to remain by your side at all times."

Raj was puzzled. Was he being arrested?

To bring an end to this farce being played, Raj allowed Kanaiyalal in and closed the door. "Are you here to arrest me, you kutte ki aulaad (spawn of a dog)"

Kanaiyalal was in the highest ranks of the Bansban state's military not without a reason. The man had tough skin. Undaunted by the young prince's tirade, he bowed and with a great show of regret said, "Bapu Saheb, your safety is solely my concern as ordained by Maharaja Saheb. I'm honored he has expressed confidence in me by assigning the task of escorting you safely to Bansban. Regretfully, I have to inform you that your brother Prince Pratap Sinhji has died this morning."

The news hit hard like a punch from a boxer. Raj felt dizzy and had to sit down.

Crown Prince dead? Where did that leave him? Oh my, he would now be first in line for Crown Prince and would inherit the "throne" later. Of course, he could decline the offer. In that case Nirmal Sinh, the third son would become king. But why should Bapu decline? If for nothing else, he would accept it merely to reek havoc on this slimy sycophant, Kanaiyalal and others who have defamed his family for centuries. Yet, Raj didn't feel sorry for his brother's death. They were strangers separated by an age gap of ten years, living in different districts and had different mothers. Ironically, this untimely demise would change so many eqquations.

Raj regained his composure as Kanaiyalal offered him a glass of water. "Are you alright, Sir?"

Raj ignored the man's offer and silently put his things inside a small suitcase. He did not forget the black & white photo of the eighteen-year-old girl who he would later seek her hand in marriage. "Excuse me, Kanaiyalal. I have some private matters to attend to. Give me a few minutes."

"Yes, Sir."

Raj wrote letters to the supervisor of the hostels, the Principal of the College and his close buddy, Mayank explaining his sudden departure. He then came out seeing Kanaiyalal waiting.

"You may lead the way."

* * *

Raj sat alone in the back seat along the way to Bansban and continued thinking from where he had left. Once again, he remembered that young sweet Desi and resumed jerking off. Two minutes later, he ejaculated inside his silk handkerchief just as the car was entering the main gate of Darbar Gad. No one looked back and Raj didn't care if they did. Darbar Gad was a fortress enclosure that covered five acres of land and in its center, stood a three-story building housing the Royal Family. This day, the flag overhead flew at half-mast.

As soon as they parked, Raj rushed to see Maharaja, his brother-in-law, in his private chambers. Queen Kusum Devi, the third wife was also present; her eyes red and swollen because she cried so much. As per custom, Raj bowed and touched his elders' feet. They blessed him putting their hands above his head. Maharaja lifted him up embraced him and then broke down in tears. The Queen then followed crying loudly. The men who were present, including Kanaiyalal, sniffled and patted their eyes; forced to do so lest their eyes shall be cut out.

Raj spent half an hour with the Maharaja and then went to his mother, Saroja Devi. He touched her feet and she ran her hand across his face and over his head. Kanaiyalal stood by desiring to take Prince Raj directly to the State Offices but Raj's mother, told him sharply, "Bapu Saheb will accompany you at his pleasure. Now wait outside until summoned."

"Yes, my Queen." Kanaiyalal then closed the door.

"You must be hungry, my son. Come, the food is ready."

Raj was more in a hurry to tell his mother about the girl he had met. But the Queen would not stop talking about him being the next Crown Prince and all its implications. Raj did not get a chance to utter his thoughts.

Meanwhile, Raj's best friend Chandrakant had learned of his friend's arrival. He had personally delivered a message on Raj's behalf to the college girl earlier in the day informing her that Raj had a death in the family and would be back soon. Normally, Chandrakant would have just walked in but not today. He was denied access by Kanaiyalal, himself.

"Good riddance," he uttered as he was turned away.

It was close to midnight before Prince Raj Khatir had finally made it to bed. Once again, he thought back to his first encounter with the Desi and instantly got stimulated. He jerked off to an even stronger orgasm and then retired for the evening.

CHAPTER 1

The following five days were hectic what with the arrival of the body of Raj's brother and the customary funeral arrangements. Citizens and dignitaries swarmed to express their condolences while Raj was busy getting familiar with the office of the Crown Prince, being instructed by a bevy of State officials by the hour.

On his tenth day of being back, Prince Raj waited for the dust to settle. He proceeded in the morning after breakfast to tell his mother the story about the young desi at his university. His best friend Chandrakant, put his hand over his mouth as Raj spoke.

While Raj returned on campus after a weekend getaway,

he'd usually bring some schoolwork to keep himself busy (which was a lie). Raj told his mother about the midterms and how important they were that he didn't have a chance to enjoy his entire weekend. With nothing to do, he sat alone in his dorm room between studying, watching a cricket match and playing video games on his phone.

Earlier in the day, Raj woke up early before sunrise. After showering, he felt like going for a horse ride and called for his men to bring one. He then set out alone as the sun was beginning to rise.

There was a large plantation with sugarcane and other crops covering more than 300 acres as he passed through a forest. Raj's horse trotted away at a medium pace as the trail between the forest and the fields was rough, narrow and difficult to navigate. Suddenly the stallion faltered and Raj halted it, perking up his ears to listen to a distant whinny of another horse. His stallion answered with a mighty neigh and suddenly set off quickly, almost throwing Raj over. The horse was uncontrollable rushing into a small clearing and suddenly came to a halt. Raj couldn't prevent himself from falling and flipped directly on his butts. Luckily, the ground was wet and covered with grass; lest he'd be injured.

Before he could regain his posture, a young girl in

choli skirt and odhani rushed to him saying, "Oh, my God. What happened? Are you all right? Are you hurt?"

The girl gave him her hand and Raj gingerly sat up. Her hand felt so warm and Raj was amazed at it while continuing to hold on. "I'm alright. No broken bones. Who are you?"

Raj saw her reluctance while withdrawing her hand. He went back to the ground still feeling the pain on his buttocks. The girl replied, "Priya. My name is Priya, Bapu Saheb. Give me few minutes and I will return."

"Please, my dear. Don't ever leave a hurt man in such dire circumstances!"

"I won't."

Raj then made up some things about what happened after that but in the back of his mind, the story was far from over. As his mother spoke, Raj started having flashbacks about what did really happen.

CHAPTER 2

*L*ooking around, Raj took the stock of his surroundings. A few feet away, stood a mare tied to a tree. His stallion was now by her side nuzzling and licking her while restlessly prancing around. Raj stallion's two-foot-long dick, was now hanging and swaying like a thick black rope.

The mare tried heading towards them but realized she was still tied to the tree. Raj's stallion reared on his hind legs and mounted the mare. The mare was frightened and tried moving away from under him. The stallion's dick had stiffened to a rigid rod and was poking the mare's rear end finding her neighs. The mare was skittish and couldn't remain still as the stallion had to keep moving along with her to remain mounted. The mare was being uncooperative, so the stallion dismounted. The mare lowered her haunches and let out a mighty stream of urine. The stallion putting his nose in her privates then lifted his head skywards retracting his upper lip. His dick again was poking out and thumped against his belly.

When the stallion had a second go at the mare, the girl had just returned to help him. She had held mare's tail out of the way. As soon as the stallion mounted, the girl grabbed his dick and directed towards mare's vulva. A couple of powerful thrusts and the stallion's dick was buried to the hilt in the mare's moans.

Meanwhile, Raj looked on in amazement fantasizing the dirty things he would do to this young girl if he had the opportunity. (He didn't tell his mother his inner thoughts.)

The stallion stopped moving, keeping his dick buried in the moans. His massive head was resting on the mare's neck as it also stood quietly. After about a minute or so, the stallion dismounted. His now-shortened dick slipped out of mare's vulva as his white cum seeped out of the mare's vulva. Priya lead the stallion to another tree and tied him. She then came back to Raj and once again offered her hand to help him up. Raj took her hand but instead of him getting up he pulled her down. She lost balance and fell on his thighs.

Raj, in his twenty-one years, had never had a chance of holding a female. Inexperienced as he was, he did not know what to do. In fact, he was little apprehensive believing that the girl may slap him.

But she didn't; neither did she remove her hand from his. He opened his thighs a little and her heavy hips settled between them. Her face was flushed pink and was performing the difficult task of biting his lower lip and smiling, at the same time. Her body felt delicate and her skin felt velvet-smooth. There was a kind of intoxicating aroma coming from her.

Priya already knew him as one of the Princes but didn't know if he was from Bansban. She had seen him on several occasions but from a distance. This was the first time that Priya was having a close look at him, a real fantasy in such circumstances. As for Prince Raj Khitar, he looked to the tee. He was tall, hefty with a broad muscular chest and a tattoo on his right shoulder. He had the darkest eyes with jet black hair. His lips were chiseled and adorned by a thin line of mustache below his straight sharp nose.

So, when he pulled her down into his lap Priya almost died of shyness. This was the one of whom her friends were always talking in fascination. He was looking at her in a way that made her cringe. And his hand that was holding hers, it was so big and thick!

"How would that hand feel rubbing her pussy?" she thought.

Priya suddenly became aware of his face approaching hers. Was he going to kiss and take her virginity?

Raj lowered his face towards hers and she avoided the impending kiss by averting her face at the last second. His lips crash-landed on her ear. He kissed there, nibbling and murmured, "Priya, Priya. How sweet is your name! It befits you. You are as sweet as the mare." Raj kissed her again and goosebumps broke out on her body but not literally. These kisses caused her to giggle.

With a toothy smile accompanied by two dimples on her cheeks, Priya grabbed Raj's nose. "Liar! You tell the same thing to every girl you … Oh my! You-you are turning me on. Stop," Priya stuttered.

"What other girls?"

"Bapu Saheb, I know you are the Prince of Bansban. You must have enjoyed with so many girls."

"Priya, I swear on your name, I have not touched any girl. You are my first and the only one I desire."

Priya giggled once again and tried half-heartedly to get up from his lap, saying, "Let me go, Bapu. If somebody sees us like this, nothing will happen to you but my father will sure kill me."

Holding her down, Raj replied, "Who's your father?"

" Thakur Mangal Sinh Bharav."

"Oh, so you come from the other village. Why did you have to bring the mare for mating? Your father could have sent her with a servant. Usually the young girls are not put to such tasks. How old are you?"

"Bapu, we are very poor and cannot afford a servant. Beside, my father himself is serving some-body. The mare has been in heat for two days and was quite miserable last night. So, I took it upon myself when my father had to go to his work to find a mate. And yes, I turned eighteen last month."

"Are you not embarrassed?"

"Not really. What about you?"

"I'm not embarrassed, I'm excited. Can you not feel the proof of my excitement?"

In fact, Raj was having a hard-on of a lifetime. His dick was pleasantly pressed against Priya's buttocks and he made it jerk. "Do you see?"

Priya felt so shy that she averted her face looking downward. She could not however, control her smile. "Bapu Saheb, please let me go. I'm afraid of myself. I do not want to do anything, which would bring disgrace to our families. Let me go, please."

As she spoke, Raj had been holding her hand and playing with her fingers. He reluctantly released it and Priya got up off his lap. He remained seated. She stood near him with her back to him. Raj gazed at her smooth legs, trim ankles and dainty little feet below the hem of her short skirt. How nice it would feel to caress those feet! His dick jerked discharging a small amount of pre-cum in his pants.

Priya glanced briefly over her shoulder and started walking towards her mare in slow dejected steps. Her rounded hips were swaying and juggling enticingly.

And Raj had to have her, no matter what, even

if he had to temporarily marry her. The Mataji would not object because of her poverty as she came from the reputable Rajput family. Raj envisioned he would make love to her daily and have many children. They would have a big house, cars and many servants and would be source of envy to many others. Golden days were ahead and Raj had to have her for sure.

Deep inside, he felt in his heart an overpowering feeling for Priya the like of which he had never experienced for anybody else. "Call her, you fool, call her before she goes away," his heart said.

And call he did. He got up and shouted, "Priya, wait. I love you, my dear. Will you marry me?"

Priya stopped in her tracks and slowly turned around as if not sure of what she heard. Raj invited her with pleading eyes and outstretched arms. She did not hesitate for a second. With tear-stained face, Priya ran the short distance and flung herself in the arms of her new Prince. Hiding her face in his chest, she bawled away. Raj held her tight, feeling her firm breasts crushed on his chest. His hands caressed her back going up and down, soothing her while he kissed her head.

Putting a finger under Priya's chin, Raj lifted

her face and wiped her tears. Then, he whispered, "I love you, my dear."

Priya tightened her grip around him and replied in a hushed tone, "I love you too, Pyare. Oh my Prince, why do I like you so much that my heart aches?"

"Because I love you so much."

Overwhelmed, Priya pulled his face down to a kiss. Raj found her lips so soft and sweet that he took over and kissed her again and again and again.

* * *

Both had no experience and didn't know how to proceed. Tentatively, Raj pressed his lips on Priya's and brushed them from one end of her mouth to the other. Priya's lips opened up of their own and Raj breathed in her sweet breath. So fragrant! His dick bobbled a couple of times and became harder with each instance.

Now, Raj imitated Priya and opened. For a moment, an open mouth was stuck to an open mouth and nothing else happened. Then, Raj sucked Priya's lower lip between his and wetted it. Tremors that burst out from hers ran to her nipples and vulva. She responded back by mashing her mouth on his. Her hips involuntarily pushed against his body causing Priya to now feel the hardness of Raj's dick.

Frantic kissing between them became uncontrollable. Nobody knows how and when it happened, but their tongues joined the fray and soon a simple kiss turned into torrid French-kissing. Surprisingly, it was Priya whose tongue was first to invade. It ran all around and dueled with Raj's tongue causing him to suck on hers like a lollypop.

When Priya pulled her tongue back, Raj took his turn. When he tried entering, Priya playfully clamped her mouth shut. Raj ran his tongue along the length of her closed lips and tried to pry them open. She denied access and Raj separated himself gazing into her mischievous eyes. Seeing his face, Priya couldn't contain herself from laughing.

As soon as her mouth opened again, Raj descended like a hawk and captured it. He forced his tongue inside and ran it along to all the corners and Priya finally welcomed the invasion. She felt the stimulations coursing down her body before settling in her pussy area. She was surprised and embarrassed to feel her bhos (vulva) getting heavy and sticky. There was a strange throb now occurring in her privates. By the time Raj broke the kiss for a breather, she was feeling weak at the knees.

Priya's mouth was swollen and wet and her breasts felt tight and heavy as her nipples erected. She was hanging on and one of Raj's arms were around her waist. His other was roaming over her back from her neck above to her hips below. Time and again, he grabbed her buttocks, squeezing them and pulled her closer against his manhood. Priya felt the pulsating dick just above her vulva.

Raj's heart was racing, desperately wanting to fuck. His dick had almost reached the point of cumming. He knew Priya was ready from the way she was kissing and pushing against his dick. However, Raj had a kind of different feeling for this Desi, clearly different from mere lust. He did not want to use her just once and throw her away; he wanted to keep her and make love to her again and again. Raj wanted Priya around him day and night and visualized seeing her sleeping in his arms. He wanted to wake every morning into her smile. He mentally decided he had to fuck her now and then marry her as soon as possible.

Raj sat down on a soft patch of land covered in grass and took Priya into his lap. She sat crosswise with her back supported by his partly bent leg. Her legs, also partly bent at the knees were thrown across Raj's. Raj's left arm was around her shoulders while the right one was free while Priya's right arm encircled his chest.

Raj took her hand in his and brought it to his lips. One by one, he kissed all her fingers, one by one putting them in his mouth and sucking. At last, he kissed her palm and then flattened it on his cheek. Leaving it there, Raj's hand went to her cheek; both of them caressing each other's. Priya looked up into his eyes and said, "You are the Prince, how will you marry me, a poor village girl?"

"I am a prince but second in line, not likely to inherit the throne, you will never be a queen. I don't wish to be a king like my father; I want to be an engineer and I'm studying for only that. Marry me, my love: we shall have a big house with many servants, cars and lots of children. Will you marry me, my dear? Say yes, please."

Priya's heart was racing, too. With a catch in her throat, she could barely say, "Yes, yes, yes I will marry you. You're my Krishna and I'm your

Radha. My heart says that we have been husband wife in all of our past lives."

"Therefore, I will come to your home and ask your father for your hand."

"Please, Bapu."

Not knowing what to do next, they continued doing what naturally came to mind.

Priya looked up into his eyes, held his head and pulled him down to a kiss. She opened her mouth, he opened his, lips remained sealed to lips. Nothing happened for a while. Then his tongue sneaked out like the cock of a horse coming out of its sheath and entered hers. No sooner, her mouth was filled up than she closed her lips on his tongue much like vulva of a mare closing over the cock of the stallion. They stopped once again savoring the sweet feeling of Raj's tongue in her mouth.

After a trance of several minutes, Raj withdrew from her mouth but Priya would not let him go. She kissed him and imitated him by pushing her tongue inside. Instinctively, Raj dueled tongue with the tongue and licked her lips, too. Again, Priya was lost in the kiss and did not know what Raj was doing to her.

Raj in fact was trying to undress her taking advantage of her state of pleasure. He pulled out the pallu of her odhani from the waistband of the ghaghari and bared her stomach. His hand caressed her smooth skin and went around to her lower back. While the kissing continued, he pulled her against his chest. The pressure of her firm breasts on his chest made his dick jumped a couple of times. Priya was aware of her own increased swelling and wetness.

Priya's choli was loose fitting and large in size tied on the back by three pairs of strings. The front was flat, more or less, made up of thick cloth encrusted with intricate embroidery. It effectively prevented any indication of the size and shape of her breasts. Raj was trailing his hand up and down her back from her nape to her buttocks. He came across and pulled open the strings of the choli, one at a time. Then he turned Priya aside and gently laid her flat on the grass. His hand once again moved to her stomach. As the kissing continued, the throbs of his dick did as well and so did the flow of love juices from his dick and from her bhos.

Raj then remembered having read somewhere

that virgins are very sensitive in their breasts and the man should go about gently handling them. He wanted to see how they looked but he held himself. Raj could have easily lifted up the front of the choli or could have pushed his hand underneath but he did not. Gingerly, he put his hand on the breast over the thick covering of the choli. Immediately, Priya gripped his wrist and held on.

Raj could not feel much beyond the presence of a firm swelling. All the same time, he flexed his fingers and squeezed gently a couple of times wondering if the other breast would feel same. Just when he was about to move his hand there, Priya did something pleasantly surprising.

She was holding Raj's wrist guiding his hand back to her stomach. It appeared she didn't want his hand on her breast. But not so, in fact, she wanted more. She then pushed Raj's hand up under the flap of her choli and Raj took the hint. The choli was already untied and was loosely covering her chest. Raj's hand passed under the flap and easily slid over her left breast and softly held it in his palm. A soft moan escaped from Priya's throat.

Surprised at her daring, Raj broke the kiss to look into her eyes. Priya looked for a moment, smiled coyly and hid her face in his chest.

Raj once again changed their positions. He made her lie down flat on her back while remaining on her right side.

Lifting up the front flap of her choli he uncovered both breasts. Instinctively, her hands flew there to cover them. She blushed to a deep pink and averted her face with a smile. Raj gently removed her hands. "Priya, my dearest, what a beautiful treasure you've been hiding? Look at me. You are now my beloved wife; there is no need to feel shy anymore. Here, hold something of mine while I hold something of yours."

So saying, Raj directed her hand to his dick which was inside his pants wanting to come out. Priya held it thru his boxers while he turned to her face and kissed her lips.

For Priya, Raj's kisses were enough to make her tingle all over. Over that, was his hard pulsating dick in her hand which was doing something to her pussy she had never experienced before, She was excited but had hard time warding off her shyness. This stranger was exposing and touching parts of her body, which nobody had seen or touched before. His ministrations were sweet and exciting and for no reason Priya was feeling a surge of love for this prince; the like of which she had never felt for anyone. However, she was a little scared knowing that he had every right as a royal to fuck her.

For a second, an ugly worm of doubt lifted its head. Priya regained some of her sanity. On one hand, she wanted Raj to fuck her and on the other, she did not want him to do so before marriage. He was a Prince after all, what if he made her pregnant and then forgot her? Her mind asked the question and her heart replied, "no, no, he would not do you like that, he said he loves you."

By now, Raj's fingers were roaming over the flat plains of her stomach. He had already pulled out the pallu of her odhani and hence had no difficulty in reaching the waistband of her skirt. He just touched it and returned to her chest area. After about five trials, Raj ventured to pick up the string holding the skirt and pull it to untie its knot.

As soon as the knot was undone and skirt was loosened, Raj could insinuate his fingers underneath and crawl towards Priya's vagina area. Priya immediately caught his wrist and held him. Breaking the kiss she pleaded, "Pyare, meri ek binati maniye. (Dear, grant me one request.) Vahan chhuiye mat. (Do not touch there.)"

"Why? You like my touch, don't you?"

"Oh, dearest, I like everything about you, but I would like to keep something for our suhaag raat."

Raj's dick was so hard that he couldn't think straight. He thought about ignoring Priya and she would have to obey his command, but he had feelings for her, which he could not explain. So, he backed away, kissing her and said, "Your wish is my command, my Queen. I will wait as long as you want."

Priya in the meantime was playing with his dick still inside his boxers. She asked, "Meanwhile, what will you do with this?"

"They say that it is not healthy to leave the privates unsatisfied after arousal. Therefore, I will make it come out later this evening."

Now, Priya had heard from her married friends the facts about erections, orgasms, ejaculation, and semen but never had a chance to experience them. Somewhat out of curiosity and excitement, she lowered her gaze and said, "Can I help you in doing so?"

Raj was overjoyed, replying, "Yes, my lady. You can. It will give me great pleasure."

Red in face due to shyness, Priya opened Raj's boxers, pushed her hand in and grabbed and tried pulling it out. Poor girl, she did not know that it is difficult to take out. Her hands got wet and slimy from its pre-ejaculation. However, Raj's dick refused to come out.

Raj unbuttoned his pants and his rampant dick jumped out in Priya's hand. A pleasant thrill passed thru her when she wrapped her fingers around it. They could hardly cover half the length of the shaft.

Raj was eight inches long and two inches thick at the root. Drenched with its own juices, the bulbous head was peeping out from under the foreskin. The shaft was straight, thinnest near the head and increasing in thickness towards the root. The bag below was wrinkled dark skin housing two heavy rounded balls. The bag and the root were covered with springy black hairs.

Feeling the dick in her hands was not without effect on Priya. Her vagina and clit throbbed uncontrollably and her vulva spewed out cream.

She was strongly tempted to spread her legs and receive in that beautiful specimen. Somehow, she retained some degree of sanity and was able to curb her naughty thoughts.

Raj put his hand over her hand and moved it up and down. Priya was amazed at the slick motion of the delicate skin over its rock hard core; the swelling of the mushroom shaped head with each stroke of her hand; at the foreskin, which could be pulled up the shaft so much that the dick revealed its circumcision. Raj showed her a trick of milking the dick in the fist while stroking up and down.

Within minutes, Raj's dick was being jerked repeatedly and swelled to the extreme. Suddenly, it ejected a jet of semen high in the air; partly landing on Priya's face and chest. The first jetstream was followed in quick succession by four others of lesser intensity.

Priya watched this fascinated. She felt Raj's dick deflating rapidly in her hand. Raj wiped her face and chest with his silk handkerchief. "Similar things can be done to a girl like you. She could be brought to an orgasm without entering her moans. Let me try."

A wave of shyness once again engulfed Priya thinking as to what Raj would do to her. She couldn't look in his eyes let apart saying yes or no. Luckily, Raj made her sit on his lap with her back faced him. He kept her legs straight between his. Passing one hand under the choli, he gently held one breast with the thumb on the nipple. The other hand went to the shirt-covered private area.

Even when the touch was through clothes, Priya jumped as soon as his fingers touched it. Her legs pulled up and she grabbed her wrist. Raj did not stop as he continued caressing the vulva. After few strokes he said, "Dear, let me do what is necessary. Please do not grab my hand."

"Ok, Bapu Saheb. Please don't hurt me."

He put his hand on Priya's knee and slid upwards along the inner side of her thigh. For a moment, her thighs clamped together but soon relaxed. When his fingers reached her vulva, he found it swollen and drenched in its own creaminess. He was not conversant with the layout of vulva and hence his fingers were lost in thick bush of silky hair and her slippery labia. Somehow, he managed to locate the central slit and ran a finger along it. Priya could not hold her pelvis from rocking which further added to Raj's difficulties. Wary of injuring her privates, Raj gently pushed the finger deeper in the moist crack and continued running it back and forth. This time when he touched a spot at the front end, causing Priya to strongly jump up and grab his wrist to remove his finger. He knew that he had unknowingly bumped with her clitoris.

When Priya relaxed, Raj resumed caressing her vulva. He now carefully avoided direct contact with her clitoris which apparently was highly sensitive.

At the back end of her crack, Raj's finger slid into tight warm channel of Priya's pussy. She could easily take two fingers in despite being a virgin. About an inch deep, he felt the thin barrier of her hymen. He did not go any further. Instead, making gentle in-and-out movements of the fingers, Raj finger-fucked her for some time tormenting the clitoris by stroking its erect shaft without touching the tiny head. Priya, minutes later, had a wonderful orgasm.

Once her shaking subsided, Raj tried once more, "Shall we do like horse and the mare?"

Priya lovingly declined and Raj did not pursue the matter further. Entwined in each others arms, they continued talking and kissing for a long period. Then Priya suddenly said, "It is almost noon time and I must go. Please do not delay in seeing my father. He comes home in the evenings."

"Ok, my love."

"Here, would you like to have these?" Priya gave Raj two black and white photos of herself.

Raj took it, kissed it and said, "Now, I will not feel lonely."

They kissed and kissed and reluctantly parted ways.

A telegram was waiting for Raj when he reached home later that afternoon. He was urgently called back to College to do his midterms that happened to be starting the next day. With that, Prince Raj had no time to see Thakur Mangal Sinh, father of Priya. He called in his best friend, Chandrakant and after making him take the oath of secrecy, Raj left a message for Priya requesting her to be patient until his exams were finished. In the evening, he took leave of his mother, touched her feet and was driven to his one-room abode in his school's hostels.

The exams were rigorous and lasted for three days. On the fourth, Raj had to deal with that bitch of an instructor and had an hour of cricket practice. While climbing the stairs to the third floor of the Hostels, he was looking forwards to going home the following morning and seeing his Priya once again.

Wearily, Raj slumped on his unmade bed, loosened his pants and pulled out his limp dick. He once again recalled his encounter with Priya and it started stiffening. Tomorrow, he told unto himself, tomorrow I will go and see her father and maybe then I will fuck her. Raj's dick was fully erect now and he was fast approaching the stage of cumming.

Then Kanaiyalal, the Karbhari, bearer of the bad news knocked on the door disturbing Raj. He informed the prince that they were leaving after sunrise and that he must prepare himself for the strenuous upcoming activities.

The Maharaja declared a ten-day period of statewide mourning. A long queue of dignitaries, both local and foreign was waiting to see Maharaja and offer condolences. Raj as prospective Crown Prince was obliged to attend with a degree proportionate to their status and importance. It was Kanaiyalal who was handling this business but Raj had to remain by his side. Then there was arrival of the deceased, its public viewing, followed by cremation; this took a whole week. In the end started the preparations for his induction as Crown Prince. All these days he was under constant surveillance in the name of safety and could not move an inch without the knowledge of that hyena, Kanaiyalal.

It's been fifteen days since Raj had a chance to talk to his mother. He told her about meeting a Rajput girl and their mutual promise of marriage. Queen Saroja Devi, his mother could easily read his pleasure on his bashful face. She rejoiced in her heart; at last her son was showing the signs of being a "man" thanks to one of those opportunistic hussies who readily spread their legs for a member of Royal family. With a smirk on her lips she asked, "Is she pregnant?"

Shocked, Raj after a moment of hesitation vehemently replied, "No, no, no, Mataji. We have done nothing of the kind."

"If that is so, what's the problem? Bapu, there will be finer girls now practically throwing themselves at your feet. We have already received proposals from about eight royal families for your hand. You must consider all the factors. You are not a common man on the street. As a Crown Prince, you will be limited in many ways; for one, the selection of the bride is one of them. It will be your duty to give our public an acceptable person as a queen."

"But Mataji, I have promised her marriage."

"Promise? Wait for six months. I bet, she'll marry some one else and forget you. She will not wait."

"I beg your pardon, Mataji, she loves me and would not—"

"If she loves you why did she not allow you to go to the last stage? You wanted to have sex? Did you not?"

"She wants to keep herself chaste for wedding night."

"Oh, the village girl wants to give you her virginity as a wedding gift?"

Raj was feeling shy and uncomfortable talking to his mother about this, so he didn't answer.

Mataji continued, "Look Bete. Wait until you are inducted as Crown Prince. All throughout my life I have prayed for you to succeed your father. Now that that chance is there would you break my lifelong dream just for a two-bit opportunistic hussy?"

Raj could not tolerate insults to Priya. Red in face, he could only say, "I beg your pardon, Mataji. May I be excused?"

Saroja Devi said, "I am sorry if I have hurt your feelings but sometimes bitter medicine is the only remedy. Think about it. You may go now."

* * *

The following day, Queen Saroja Devi received in her private quarters her dealer of precious jewels. Nobody knew of him, not even Kanaiyalal. The man from Ahmedabad worked in the Homeland Ministry of the Central Government and was spying for Queen Saroja. She'd made sure he was well taken care of in exchange. The moment he came, he told Queen Devi some bad news of the government gearing up for annexation of the states in the upcoming months. The days of Bansban as one were numbered.

Queen Saroja pondered the move replying, "But surely the rulers of these states will get something in return?"

"No, the King will receive a payout of which to

be negotiated by the Parliament. He will then disperse it among the rulers and the monarchy will be dissolved at once."

This would be a great cause of concern for Queen Saroja Devi as this would now only affect her but every state family. Yes, Raj would inherit the annuity but the throne would be no more rendering each family powerless. Therefore, the Queen decided to give Raj a heads-up; telling him to accept being Crown Prince until the annexation.

The ceremony of Raj becoming the Crown Prince was celebrated without any complications. There was religious ceremony in the morning that lasted for three hours. This was followed by a short procession ending into extravagant feast in company of selected few. Priya and Chandrakant were not invited.

The afternoon gathering was reserved for general public. Anybody could come and congratulate the new Crown Prince. Almost all the visitors came with some form of offering, waiting patiently in a long queue for their turn.

At first, Prince Raj Khatir did not recognize Priya, she had changed so much. She'd lost weight while her complexion had darkened. She appeared unkempt with hair flying in all directions and there were big black circles under her sad eyes which were red and puffy due to constant crying. Priya was carrying something wrapped in a dirty cloth which the guards presumed to be a gift but in fact was only a wad of rags.

The perpetual smile adorning the Prince's face vanished faster than a drop of water on red hot iron. Priya was staring with dry eyes as there were no tears were left to shed. Raj almost got up from his seat but restrained himself. She wordlessly put forth her hand as if begging. With difficulty, she croaked one word, "Fotu (photo)"

Sensing something unusual, the guards descended upon her like hawks, taking her by her arm and dragging her away. She continued mumbling "Fotu, mera fotu (photo, my photo.)"

Raj could not bear seeing her in this state. He immediately left the hall complaining of having a headache. He requested immediate audience with Maharaja and Queen Saroja Devi. He had to wait for an hour and was granted only five minutes.

Five minutes was too much time. When the door of

the chamber closed, Raj announced in firm voice, "Your Highness and Mataji, I respectfully request the permission to denounce my title of Crown Prince in favor of Prince Nirmal Sinh."

The King and the Queen were surprised but did not ask why. Saroja Devi at that point realized that her son was really in love with that young girl. Her heart was almost burst with compassion as she rushed to Raj and hugged him. Running her fingers through his hair she said with tears in her eyes, "Go my son, go and be happy. I'm so sorry."

Maharaja granted his wish. Raj touched their feet and rushed out like a bird freed from a cage.

A group of guards immediately surrounded him and Raj dismissed them with a curt, "I will summon you when I need you."

He left out of the palace and grabbed the horse from the nearest guard. Leaving the gawking guard, Raj raced to the neighboring village where he found out Priya's home and dismounted.

"Where is Priya?" he asked a middle-aged man who came forward to receive him.

"Welcome, Bapu Saheb. Oh oh, I am honored

by your gracious visit to our meager home. Sevak Mangal Sinh is present at your service."

"So, you are Priya's father? Where is the lady?"

"I beg your pardon, Saheb, she has gone to Bansban to greet you. Does she not meet you there?"

As he spoke, Priya arrived. "Oh, foolish girl, what in the name of God?"

A small crowd of spectators had gathered in the courtyard of the house. They parted making way for Priya. She appeared to be in a haze and was being led by two girls close to her age.

"We found her roaming the streets of Bansban," said one of them.

Walking on unsteady feet, Priya barely made to the doorsteps and collapsed.

Raj was quick. He jumped and gathered her in his arms before she hit the ground. He landed jarringly on his side cushioning Priya. Mangal Sinh came up and lifted Priya to the charpoy near by. Somebody brought in water to sprinkle on her face. Within minutes, she opened her eyes.

Raj was hovering above her and Priya asked in a weak voice, "What happened? Where am I, Pyare?"

"You are with me, darling. You fainted. Are you ready to marry, my love?"

"Yes, Bapu Saheb.'

Raj then asked her father for Priya's hand and later in the day, they were married at the family home.

CHAPTER 5

*E*arlier that dreadful day at Priya's home, weak tired and disheveled Priya had shamelessly thrown her arms around Raj's neck and continued chanting "Don't leave me, Pyare. Mujhe apani daasi bana lijiye lekin chodiye mat (Make me your servant but do not abandon me).

Embarrassed to see his daughter this way, Mangal Sinh took up the task of dispersing the crowd. When Priya settled in sleep, Raj in presence of couple of other gents and ladies formally asked Mangal Sinh of Priya's hand in marriage making it clear that he no longer was the Crown Prince.

Mangal Sinh conferred with the elders present and accepted the proposal. For the desire of fancy sweets, they distributed gud and Raj asked for their leave. The ladies would not have it and prepared some traditional sweet dishes and treated Raj with a nice loving dinner befitting of a son-in-law. Poor, yet they were great hosts.

As they ate, Raj sent word for his family's physician to be immediately dispatched to check Priya's condition. Luckily, there was nothing which could not be remedied with few days of rest and food.

Within two hours, Queen Saroja Devi, back at the palace, had cleared the financial affairs of Mangal Sinh and gifted him several acres of land and a decent house in a nearby village.

Prince Nirmal Sinh officially assumed the title of Crown Prince and his mother gifted Raj with a modest bungalow on the outskirts of city of Surat. Raj had his best friend, Chandrakant enroll Priya at his school and upgraded his accommodations at the college's hostels to be closer to her. He expected that Priya would come over after school every day so he could fuck her whenever he wanted.

Meanwhile, Raj was having his new bungalow in Surat prepared for their honeymoon. In the back of his mind, he knew that the title of Crown Prince would be over in a matter of weeks.

CHAPTER 6

The day of the marriage had been hectic, who were being invited to lunch and to dinner, friends and guests coming and going, some religious ceremonies and visit to some of the nearby temples. Despite all the activities, Priya remained foremost on Raj's mind. Again and again, he reminisced their guilty encounters and fantasized as to what he would do tonight. He remembered the wonderful feel of her soft body in his arms, of her firm breasts on his chest and her delicious lips on his lips. His dick started erecting. By evening, Raj was so perked up that he himself was scared of his blinding passion and had 'relieved' himself twice to dampen his ardor. His dick proved to be rebellious, remaining semi-erect when not fully.

Priya was no better off. Her Prince was not away from her thoughts for a second. As if her own memories of past and fantasies of the future were not enough to keep her pussy wet and swollen. Some of her closest friends were bent upon telling her in unclear words as to what her Prince was likely to do to her and how she should surrender herself. Also, was the fear of unknown, of pain of the first entry and the perpetual question of every bride: would she be able to please her beloved? She had not forgotten the feel of his fingers on her breasts and his tongue on her lips. Her palms still tingled on remembering the feel of his long dick in her hands. Much against her wish, her pussy continued getting suffused and salivating in spite of several washings.

At long last, it was evening time. The beautician claimed her for a whole two hours. Priya was then led to their bedroom by few of her cousins and closest friends all giggling and laughing.

The room was large and lavishly decorated, thanks to Crown Prince Nirmal Sinh. There were flowers all around. The bed was big enough for four adults covered with satin bed sheets, strewn liberally with red rose petals. There was the usual furniture and soft lights. A French door led to a small balcony outside and a similar small door on the other side opened into a palatial bathroom replete with all modern equipment.

The unique feature of the room however was the presence of mirrors; mirrors everywhere including the ceiling above the bed.

That is where Raj found her when he in turn was escorted by the same group of rowdy females. He closed the door in their faces, locked it and turned around to face Priya.

His heart missed several beats. She looked so ravishingly beautiful sitting demurely dressed in choli ghaghari of white silk with covering of saffron-colored transparent odhani. Besides the traditional menhdi on her hands and feet, Priya had mangal sutra in the neck, bengals on the wrists and anklets at the ankles. A thick strand of mogra flowers was braided in her hair. This appeared to be an entirely different Priya from whom he had seen before.

Raj was no less handsome. He was lean five feet eight weighing 160 pounds. He had deep wide chest and slim waist. His limbs resembled a rugby player. His face had chiseled features with black eyes and black hair. Elegantly dressed in kurta pajamas, he looked a Prince. Priya's heart raced and she felt weak in her knees.

Upon entering the room, Raj took a coupe of steps towards the bed and stopped. Priya was sitting looking downward. Raj stared at her till she lifted her gaze to meet his. Then, he smiled and spread his arms.

Despite her shyness Priya hurriedly got off the bed and ran in his arms. Throwing her arms around his chest she hugged him tightly, flattening her breasts on his chest. He gathered her with his hands on her waist. Nuzzling his head on her shoulder, Raj whispered in her ear, "I love you, I love you, I love you."

Her heart swelled. With a voice weak with excitement she said, "I love you too, my Prince."

Feeling of her soft pliable body in his arms awakened his arousal. Her pussy also got engorged and wetter. She could feel his hardening dick near her stomach and involuntarily she grinded against it.

Goose bumps erupted all over Priya's body. She turned her face up, eyes closed and lips quivering. From her waist, one of Raj's arm went up between her shoulders, the other descended to her rounded buttocks and pulled her closer. Holding her firmly,

Raj lowered his head to kiss her. He breathed in her fragrant breath and touched lips with the lips.

It was a brief kiss but very intoxicating causing sparks through Priya's body. Raj's dick stepped up to next higher level of arousal.

Raj felt a strong urge to throw this bride of his flat on the bed, lift up her ghaghari and simply ravish her by ramming her luscious walls. Remembering that she was a virgin, Raj held himself and decided to go easy.

To allay her fears, if any, he whispered, "Don't be afraid, my Dove. I will be very gentle in making love to you. Remember, I promised you before marriage? Have I kept my promise?"

Priya looked up into his eyes and said, "Yes, my dear."

"Now that we are married you will allow me to make love to you?"

She surely would, she was eager and ready. But there was something comical in the way he asked her or in the words he used that made her feel funny. Priya could not help but burst out into peals of laughter. Covering her mouth, she looked up to him with a sparkle of mischief in her eyes and shook her head.

Raj was astonished. Did she say no? He smiled

and asked again, "No? Did you say no?"

Giggling behind her fingers she averted her face and said, "Yes, I said no." Playfully, Priya took out her hand, grabbed his dick and palmed it.

From the glint in her eyes and her blatant gesture, Raj knew she was being playful. He however did not want to play games; he wanted to fuck. With effort, he controlled his urge and joined her game to please his beloved wife.

Showing mock anger on his face he said menacing, "Girl, you have not seen the wrath of my fury. Let me remind you that it is your wifely duty to submit yourself to me your lawfully wedded husband. If you don't do it willingly, I will take you by force."

That was what Priya wanted, being taken, being molested, being fucked with or without force. But she continued with the game and shook off his hands when he tried to touch her face. Tweaking his nose she countered, "You dare not."

Raj said in a voice gruff with excitement, "I will show you." and grabbed her by her shoulders. She shook his hands off. He tried again and she shook off again. Little skirmish ensued, he tried to catch her while she tried to escape. Both were laughing and giggling. Raj could easily have subdued her and for a while, thought of overpowering this delicate girl, spreading her thighs and ramming his dick up her pussy. But his heart said no and sanity prevailed. He allowed her to play the game known as 'hard to get'.

They were standing with Priya's back towards the bed, He walked her backward till her knees touched the bed. Suddenly, Raj gave her a powerful shove and threw her flying on the bed with her legs high and wide in the air. She landed unceremoniously on her back with her skirt almost to her waist exposing her smooth reddish thighs and pussy in between.

Before Priya could recover from the shock, Raj threw himself on her pinning her with his weight. She writhed and thrashed with all her might trying to throw him off. She did not gain anything. The struggle only led to further widening of her legs, further riding up of her skirt and further unveiling of her pussy.

Raj caught her wrists and pulled her arms above her head gripping the head in between the upper arms, settling at the same time in the cradle of her open thighs. His pelvis pressed against hers. He rocked it pushing his dick in the crack of her wet and swollen pussy. Waves of sweet tingling sensations burst forth from her spreading all throughout her body. Priya's struggle lost the wind and she melted as her excitement escalated.

She lost the battle but not the spirit. In defiance, she did what a schoolgirl would do: pulled out her large tongue to him and burst out laughing. With the glint in her eyes which is seen only in the eyes of a girl ready to be fucked, Priya licked her lips and pouted them provocatively for a kiss.

Raj slowly lowered his head to kiss. When he was millimeters away, she suddenly jerked her face away and Raj landed on her neck. Bent upon, now, to capture her mouth, Raj chased it while Priya kept evading him turning her head every other way.

Eventually it was Priya who got tired. She yielded to her husband's demand and accepted his mouth in kiss. She opened her mouth for him to enter. Even, as she was sucking his tongue she grabbed Raj's dick and gave it a tight squeeze.

That action of hers broke the dam causing Raj to lose control.

Raj suddenly went berserk. Blinded by raw lust he forgot his plan of leisurely love making, forgot the tenderness of her virgin pussy, forgot her hymen and forgot about himself. Pent up passions burst forth and he became oblivious to the world.

Like a man possessed, he grabbed her jaw in his grip digging his fingers in Priya's soft cheeks. He mashed his mouth with hers bruising her delicate lips with his teeth. He practically devoured her mouth and forced it open with his fingers, As if he was punishing her for some crime, he thrust his tongue down her throat making her gag.

His hands flew everywhere. He mercilessly attacked her tender breasts, grabbing them, mauling them and pinching the delicate nipples to soreness.

Next moment the same hand was stroking her labia, her clit and her mons.

Roughly he spread her thighs and came down between them, His hips were already undulating trying to push the dick in. The bulbous knob of the head knocked on her mons, her clit and her labia but slithered away on the wet and slippery vulva; it could not find the mouth of her entrance. The more he failed, the more he became anxious. He started grumping groping and grabbing frantically to find vagina for his dick which would otherwise explode any minute.

Raj was lost to the word but Priya was not. She was practically crushed under his weight. However, she was delighted to have him covering her with that much passion. She found his love making a bit rough but she welcomed it because it was apparently giving both of them so much pleasure. Volleys of electrifying thrills ran up her spine to invade the rest of her body. Her pussy tingled, her clit danced, and her vagina throbbed. Hence, though Priya was a bit apprehensive, she cooperated with him by spreading her thighs wide and tilting to bring her pussy forward for easy penetration.

Raj was becoming impatient by seconds, anxious to bury his dick inside. Priya was craving to get her vagina stuffed by its mightiness. He on his own was not getting anywhere. So, she did with Raj what she had done with the stallion on that fateful morning, She held his wayward cock and brought it to the right spot.

Not knowing what he was doing, Raj instinctively gave one powerful thrust with his pelvis and sent his rampant cock to the deepest reaches of her vagina, tearing her hymen on its way.

Priya felt excruciating pain. A sharp scream from her throat awakened Raj. He froze out of blinding fear.

His heart sank when he saw her face, pale and covered with thin sheen of perspiration. Her body was stiff like a board and her breathing labored. He dared not move his dick.

Stroking gently, he asked with genuine concern, "Are you alright my dear? Oh, my God, what have I done? Open your eyes, my love."

Presently she opened her eyes and said in a voice weak due to pain, "Pyare, it hurts."

"Oh my dear, I am sorry. I was carried away and gave you so much pain. You want me to pull out?"

"Are you in?"

"Yes, my dear."

"Then do not pull out, please. Only do not move for some time."

He showered thousand kisses on her face and said, "Forgive me, please forgive me."

It was difficult for him to remain immobile with his dick buried in her teenage walls. For one thing, it was a tight fit, the dick being thick for her narrowness. Secondly, her pain was fast decreasing and the vagina had started throbbing, gently caressing the sensitive head. Intense pleasure was being built up in her as his dick was pushing them both towards an orgasm even without moving.

* * *

True to his Rajput blood Raj 'held down the fort', though not without effort. Eventually, the pain disappeared. Priya regained her color and spirit. She smiled, ran her fingers on her Prince's worried eyebrows and said, "Do not worry, Bapu Saheb. You do not have to apologize, the pain was inevitable. I'm glad that you're the one giving me that pain. I love you."

Raj was greatly relieved seeing Priya regaining color. The pressure of his dick was becoming unbearable. He felt that he would cum soon even if he did not move.

He said, "My dear, I am going to start thrusting. Let me know if you feel so much as slightest discomfort."

With a smile on her face Priya said, "Okay."

Gingerly Raj pulled out about two inches. No pain. He waited for few seconds and equally carefully pushed it back in. No pain again.

Second time he pulled out three inches and sunk in slowly. Not only there was no pain but also her vagina spasmed when he re-entered.

It took all of his power of restrain to fuck slowly. But Raj did, with increasing length of his cock till after full ten minutes, he could stroke her vagina with almost full length. Then, he increased his speed.

Priya also was feeling the pressure mounting along with his gradual movement. Her internal muscles started throbbing and her pussy secreted large *q*quantities of cream. Her pelvis started swinging in rhythm with his thrusts.

Soon a stage was reached when he was fucking her with deep and fast strokes. However, he refrained from pushing the dick to the hilt and from pulling it completely out of her vagina. There was no bashing of mons on the mons, no entry of dick at different angles.

He fucked his beloved Priya fast but carefully for about ten minutes during which Priya did not feel any pain. She responded to his strokes by grabbing his dick and swinging in all directions.

Orgasm, when it hit came on suddenly. Priya climaxed first. Suddenly she was submerged in a huge wave of pure ecstasy. Her body stiffened in a board like rigidity only she kept jerking back and forth. Her eyes winched shut and her teeth gashed. Her nails scratched Raj's buttocks. The vagina went into a series of spasms with cream all over Raj's dick. Equally suddenly she relaxed, shuddered and slumped down as if drained off of her energy.

Raj had not stopped thrusting during her orgasm though he had changed the rhythm to slow and shallow. He could with an effort hold himself in spite of the creaminess of her pussy. However, he succumbed to the soft fluttering of her vagina during post-orgasmic period. He suddenly increased the speed and depth of his strokes fucking Priya vigorously and bringing himself on the brink of cumming.

Gathering her slender body into a vice like embrace and using the dick as a dagger, Raj stabbed her forcefully some five to six times sending the dick to the deepest recesses of Priya's vagina and plunged himself into a glorious orgasm. His dick rammed inside the vagina became longer thicker and harder than ever and shot wad after wad. Each burst was accompanied by a wave of pure bliss arising spreading all over inside.

The tempest subsided. Raj dismounted pulling out seeing his semen mixed with Priya's blood underneath the white bedside towel they were fucking on.

Raj concerned said, "Oh my dear, what did I do? I am sorry that I gave you so much pain. I was carried away, Please forgive me.

Priya said, "Do not apologize, Pyare. This was inevitable. I'm glad it was you to give me my first."

"Does it hurt?"

"I feel some soreness but no pain. Want to do it again?"

"I need to go to bathroom. When I come back, we shall continue till morning,"

CHAPTER 7

In the bathroom, Raj peed and washed off his privates. When he pulled up the foreskin, he realized that the head had become so sensitive that his toes curled on merely touching it. The cold water took away some of its wind and it softened to flaccid state.

Raj walked out of the bathroom.

He was stark naked. Priya saw him walking to her, his soft penis undulating like a pendulum. Her heart swelled with riotous emotions of love, lust, and pride.

"This is my Prince. How handsome he looks. And he loves me," she mused.

She was mesmerized by his wilted dick. She thought, "Is this the wonderful wand which had entered me from below and transformed me from a girl to a woman? Oh, the pain it gave? And the subsequent ecstasy? Will it be as delightful again? How would it feel in my mouth?"

As if reading her thoughts Raj asked, "Do you like what you see?"

Priya nodded in the affirmative. She said, "It looks so innocent."

"You can do with it what you like."

Gingerly, Priya picked up the soft penis with her fingertips and immediately felt it jump. She almost jumped it remembering the feel of his thick, erectness which Raj had taught her on that memorable morning. This penis felt so different. But wait a minute, it was getting filled up, getting thicker and harder by the millisecond. Within no time, it became fully erect, jerking every few seconds and oozing out cum from its slit.

Seeing her intoxicated with desire, Raj started disrobing his lovely bride. He removed pins from her hair to release the odhani. That done he unveiled her head and shoulders pushing odhani down to her waist. Lastly, Raj pulled out the pallu from the waistband of the ghaghari and removed the garment entirely. That left Priya clad only in choli and skirt. Turning her around, Raj pointed out their bare images in the mirror on the wall.

One look in the mirror and Priya cringed. Instantly, she covered her chest with her arms, not without a reason. The choli was more revealing than concealing. It was a tiny blouse with a plunging neck-line and no back, held in place by the sleeves and three pairs of strings tied on the back across the midline. Priya's breasts were medium size yet were seen spilling out from the low cut choli. The cloth was very thin and Priya's nipples were clearly outlined. Priya was looking extremely sexy in this outfit.

While Raj was busy in dealing with her dress, Priya was attending to his dick feeling its hot and hardness in her palm which caused her pussy tingle and discharge.

A tug of war was raging in the heart of Priya between desire and modesty. Her mounting passions gave her courage to take active part in their foreplay while the shyness held her off. As a result, one moment she would be wantonly stroking while the next, she would drop it and put up her hands to cover her breasts.

Raj, no less excited than Priya relentlessly continued undressing his bride. He reached behind her and untied the three strings holding the choli. Then he gently pushed her down flat on the bed and kissed her all over. Priya held his head and pulled him up from her breast to her mouth.

"Oh my God, Oh my God."

Sitting high on her chest each was crowned by a well-demarcated pink areola of two inches diameter with a small dainty nipple in the center. Both, the nipples and areolas were swelled up due to excitement. Delightful thrills started from the nipple and spread all over.

Raj stroked the breasts while she kissed himself all over. When Priya had enough and could not tolerate his lips on her sensitive nipples, she pulled him up.

Raj tried to open Priya's thighs but failed. He then came back to her stomach. With the flatness of his hand, he felt the smooth skin covering her abs. When his fingers touched her belly button, she jumped up and said, "It tickles. Please don't touch me there."

That gave Raj the cue. He ran his forefinger along the length of her lower lip and put it in her mouth. He played inside for some time and then took the finger to her belly button. He wetted it with her saliva and ran the finger in and around.

That was too much for Priya. She felt tickled and jumped exposing her thighs. The touch of Raj's fingers on her was like magic to Priya causing shivers to run through her body. She held her thighs again, trapping Raj's hand in between and tossed and turned to dislodge it. Her squirming did not help, on the contrary the ghaghari rode up exposing more of Priya's thighs. Eventually, she gave up and allowed Raj to spread her legs.

Priya relaxed, feeling weak with excitement. Raj straightened her legs and ran his fingers up and down her smooth thighs sliding her skirt further upwards. In the end, he lifted up the skirt right up to her waist baring both of her legs, her pussy, and everything beneath. Priya covered her privates shocked at Raj's naughtiness.

Raj marveled. Priya's fair-skinned thighs were heavy and rounded. With her legs straightened only a part of her pussy was visible. It was mainly covered by a dense growth of black silky hair extending down over the outer sides of her large labia. Only an inch of the slit was visible and it appeared sticky.

Unhurriedly, Raj untied Priya's skirt and pulled it down. The more he saw of her sexy body, the more he was excited. The awareness that her Prince found her body so exciting was equally exciting for Priya.

The theoretical knowledge gained by reading books came in handy. Raj knew without doubt what to do to pleasure his lady.

As their excitement escalated and passion piled up they appeared to be engaged in sort of a duel; and duel it was, each opponent striving to give maximum pleasure to the other. Both had thrown to winds the caution of sustaining injury. They simply fucked on, moaning and grunting with Aaahs, Uuhhs. Siiiisis. Uuiiis and such.

It was Priya who was swept into an orgasm first. Suddenly she was engulfed by the wave upon wave in the sea of pure bliss. She convulsed from head to toe, became stiff for few seconds and then relaxed completely. Her eyes got winched and saliva drooled out from her mouth. Her pussy went into a prolonged series of strong spasms accompanied by jerking and stiffening of her clitoris. It appeared that Priya had passed out again.

Raj was scared. He stopped moving with his dick almost out. He tapped her cheeks and asked, 'Are you alright my dear?' His heart sank when Priya did not respond. He kissed her shook her head and repeated. This time Priya moved a little and opened her eyes. She looked around dazed. Raj breathed and almost cried out of relief. He continued caressing her face kissing in between and asking, "Are you alright, dear?"

Priya took a couple of minutes to get herself together. Then she asked, "What happened to me? Oh Pyare, I feel like I died. The pleasure was so good. My love, is this what they call climaxing?"

"I think so."

"You did not have one, did you? I can feel your dick only it's getting soft. What will you do?"

Raj did not know what to do and say. However, he tried to fuck with semi erect cock, now moving slow and steady. He asked Priya to keep her legs closed and straight. He spread his thighs and stroked them. His dick reached a higher degree of hardness while her clitoris started throbbing again. In this position he could not push the whole length of his dick inside; only half could go in but was in constant contact with her clit stimulating it with each movement in and out. Soon, Priya's hips started swaying and jerking and Raj's dick started uncontrollable throbbing. He increased the speed and depth of his strokes knowing he was almost about to cum.

Priya spread her thighs wider and allowed him free rein of movements. In frenzy, he pounded her mercilessly and climaxed. AAAAAAHHH!!! Raj's body convulsed squashing Priya. He released five to six jets of cum, each accompanied by an exquisite thrill.

Feeling the powerful jetstreams of warmness inside her was enough to give Priya a second orgasm. Her whines were loud as Priya creamed on Raj's dick as she did before.

Raj then smothered her with a thousand kisses and Priya moved his elbows and knees she made him fully lie down on her. His weight was feeling so good that she held on him when he tried to get off her. Her hands lovingly caressed his broad back. For several minutes, they enjoyed the post-coital intimacy.

CHAPTER 8

The next morning they found themselves entwined in 'spoon' fashion, Priya being the one inside. Raj woke up first and had his usual morning hard-on making him to forget about everything else. Up to now, the first thing he was used to doing was relieving himself. From now onward, that would not be necessary; his dear Priya would do it for him.

Both laid in bed dazed by last evening's activities. Running his hand on her back, Raj was amazed at the smoothness of Priya's skin, He caressed the cheek of her butt and squeezed it. From her buttock, his fingers trinkled downward. Priya woke up when she felt her clit being massaged. She pretended to be in a deep sleep to see what Raj was up to.

To much of his delight, Raj found Priya was still wet and slippery. He inserted two fingers in the dripping and still Priya pretended to be asleep. Soon after, his dick replaced his fingers. When that happened, Priya opened the eyes and moaned. Each stroke was extremely pleasurable and she didn't want Raj to stop until he did momentarily.

"Good Morning, did you sleep well?"

"Yes, Pyare. I did. But what do I feel inside me?"

"Where?"

She contracted her inner muscles to squeeze, blushed heavily and said, "Right here."

"Oh, that? Let me pull it out and see what it is."

"No, no, " she said and pushed her hips backwards as if to engulf more of it inside her. "Whatever it is, it feels sweet. Hay, wait a minute, you cheater, is it not yours?"

"Maybe it's not. Where has this thing entered?"

"You know where, Pyare."

"How did it ended up there?"

"You started having sex with me, that's how."

"No, my dear, I started making love."

"It's still hard."

"Yes. Are you ready?"

"Anytime you command, my love, anytime."

Before Raj could bring put his manhood inside, Priya once again closed her thighs, straightened her legs and pushed Raj flat on the bed saying, "It's my turn now, Bapu."

Raj was surprised. He lied down on his back and Priya started stroking but marveling at the design. With curiosity, she lowered her head and kissed the tip running her lips over the slope. Priya then opened her mouth and swallowed it. She could not take in more than three out of eight inches. Besides the bulbous head was so big that it filled her mouth to the capacity. Priya was thrilled to feel it in her mouth and started sucking on it like a lollypop, stroking it at the same time. Several times she withdrew the cock slithering her lips over the sloping surface of the head.

The effect on Raj was predictable; he was on his way to cumming as he kept saying her name. Priya felt the pressure accompanied by rapid strong jerks --a prelude to an orgasm—and quickly removed Raj's dick from her mouth.

"Do you like it, Pyare?" she asked.

With a strained voice Raj said, "My dear, I like every thing you do to me. Oooooh! Ooooooh!" Raj's cum ejected all over Priya's face accidentally and surprisingly she didn't shy away. Raj was amazed at her innocent naughty ways as she wiped her face clean but without them licking her fingers.

* * *

They slept for most of the morning while guests remained in suspense awaiting the couples' exit. By the time they came out, it was almost high-noon.

The guests congratulated the newlyweds and some brought gifts that made Raj wonder if they were richer than him. Priya on the other hand, was immediately crowded by a group of her giggling friends and was led away to discuss her first experience. When Raj turned from waving her off, walked up upon him, his most-hated friend, Kaniyalal the Karbhari. He had just arrived with his father and mother to celebrate their sons' long-awaited matrimony.